Toad Is the Uncle of Heaven

A Vietnamese Folk Tale
Retold and Illustrated by

JEANNE M. LEE

Henry Holt and Company • New York

To the memory
of my grandmother

Henry Holt and Company, LLC
Publishers since 1866
175 Fifth Avenue
New York, New York 10010
www.HenryHoltKids.com

Henry Holt® is a registered trademark
of Henry Holt and Company, LLC.
Copyright © 1985 by Jeanne M. Lee
All rights reserved.
Distributed in Canada by H. B. Fenn and Company Ltd.

Library of Congress Cataloging-in-Publication Data
Lee, Jeanne M. / Toad is the uncle of heaven.
Summary: Toad leads a group of animals to ask the
King of Heaven to send rain to the parched earth.
[1. Folklore—Vietnam.]
I. Con cóc là câu ông trời. II. Title.
PZ8.1.L367To 1985 398.2'452787 85-5639

ISBN-13: 978-0-8050-1147-0 / ISBN-10: 0-8050-1147-1
15 14 13 12 11 10

First published in hardcover in 1985 by
Henry Holt and Company
First paperback edition, 1989

Printed in China on acid-free paper. ∞

In Vietnam, when you wish to show respect to someone, you call that person "Uncle." This old legend tells how it came to be that one day the King of Heaven called an ugly Toad "Uncle."

Once upon a time, there was a long devastating drought on Earth. Plants yellowed and withered away. Animals suffered and died. Each day, more and more living things perished, and there was no sign of rain from Heaven.

In a half-dried pond, an ugly toad struggled to live among parched lily pads.

The Toad had dug a hole in the mud. He was comfortable, protected from the scorching sun. But he was worried.

"In a few days this mud will dry, then my moist body will dry," he thought.

Then the Toad had an idea. "I must go to see the one who makes rain, the King of Heaven."

It was absurd for a toad to seek an audience with the King of Heaven; but the Toad decided he must be brave and make the trip. If he didn't, he would perish, along with all the other creatures on Earth.

The Toad hopped out of his mud hole and began the long trip to Heaven. On the edge of the pond, he saw a swarm of bees searching for nectar among the dried flowers. The Toad felt sorry for them and he stopped to talk to them.

He told them of his plan to go to the King of Heaven and ask for rain. After a quick conference, the Bees decided to go with the Toad.

The Toad hopped along, with the Bees buzzing at his side.

Passing a desolate farm, the travelers met a sad rooster who had buried his last chick that morning.

"Soon I too shall die," said the Rooster. "There is not a grain of rice anywhere. Even the farmers are starving."

When the Rooster heard of the courageous trip to Heaven, he was eager to join the group.

Through dried and dusty rice fields, they went on together. Everywhere they saw suffering and death.

At the foot of a mountain, they came upon a tired tiger, his tongue hanging out from thirst.

"I have been hungry and thirsty for so many days," complained the Tiger, "and still there is no sign of rain."

Then the Toad told him of their journey to Heaven to seek rain. Like the Rooster and the Bees, the Tiger wanted to go with them. The other animals were very glad to have such a mighty companion.

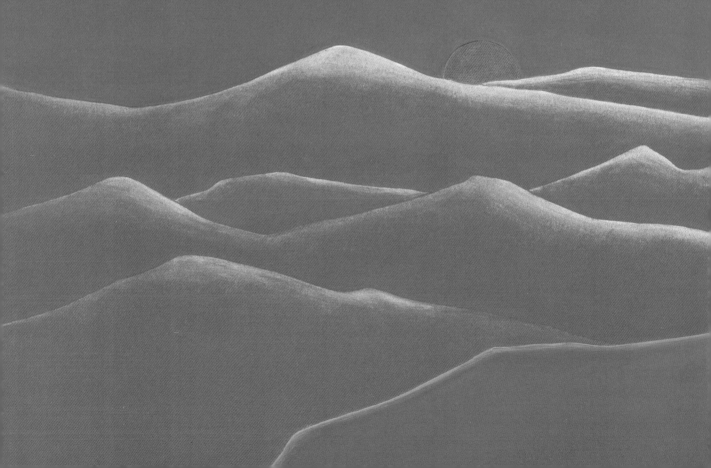

At last, they arrived at the heavenly gates. Stealthily they went in looking for the King of Heaven. They found His Majesty in a huge hall, sitting on his golden throne.

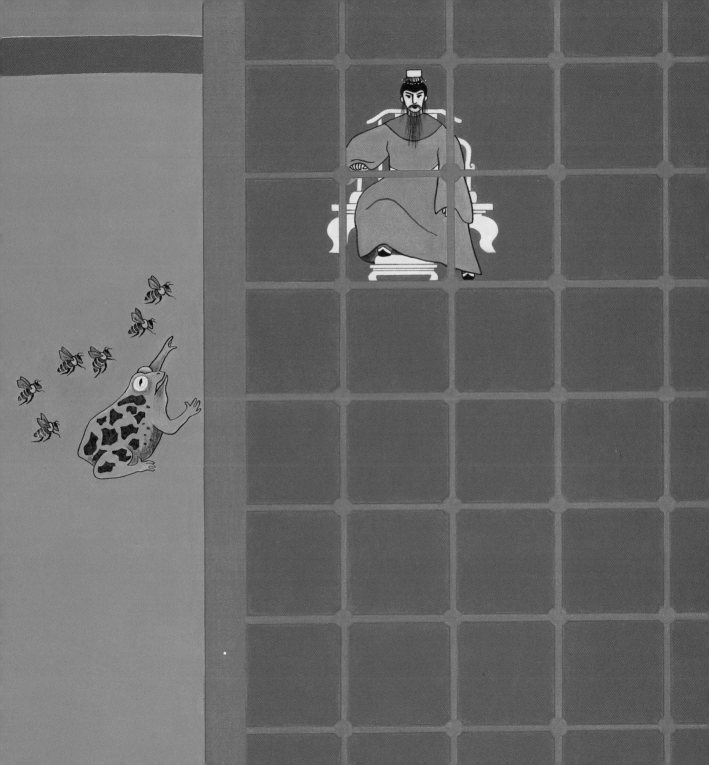

The Toad asked his friends to stand guard at the door. Then he took a long hop inside the hall.

Alas, the Toad hopped too far. Instead of landing at His Majesty's feet, he ended up in his lap.

The King of Heaven jumped up in shock.
The Toad fell to the floor. He was hurt and afraid, but he gathered all his strength and loudly croaked, "Your Majesty—"
"Guards! Seize the intruder!" shouted the King.

The Toad had just enough time to leap away while calling as loud as he could, "Bees! Bees! Help!"

The Bees flew into the hall, stinging the surprised guards. Soon the angry King was left alone with the ugly Toad and his friends the Bees. Once more the Toad gathered his courage and started to plead his case: "Your Majesty, we—"

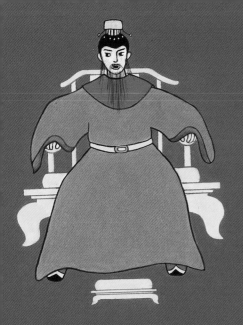

"Thunder God, quiet this impudent Toad!" ordered the King, trembling with rage.

Suddenly the whole court shook with thunder. The Rooster heard the noise and rushed into the hall.

There he let out his shrillest screech. The Thunder God dropped his drum and mallet, covered his ears, and begged the Rooster to stop.

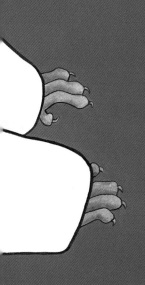

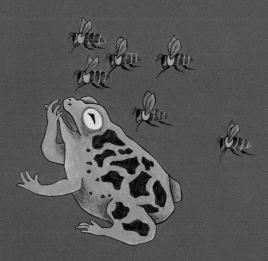

The King of Heaven could not believe his defeat. Before the Toad had a chance to collect his courage, the King bellowed, "Hound of Heaven, take these worthless animals away!"

A monstrous beast appeared. The Rooster was the first to call "Help! Help! Tiger! Quick!" while the Toad hopped around the room with the hideous hound chasing after him.

Calmly the Tiger entered.

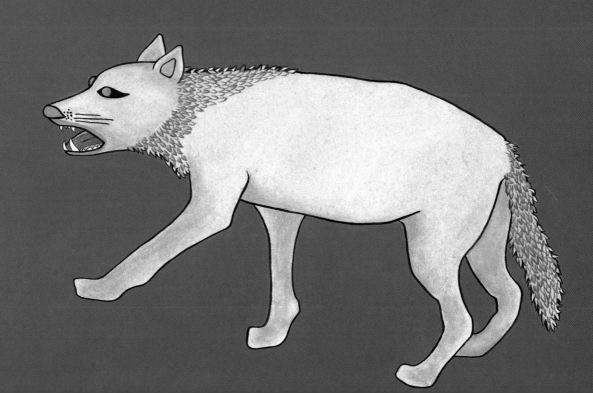

The two beasts began to fight.

Cheered on by his friends, the Tiger fought hard. Finally he held the hound under his paws and was about to sink his teeth into the beast's throat when the King of Heaven cried out, "Stop! Uncle Toad, tell your friend the Tiger to spare my hound!"

Flattered that the King of Heaven had called him "Uncle," the Toad spoke softly to the Tiger, "Let the monster go. I think His Majesty will hear us now."

The King of Heaven had indeed been respectful to the ugly Toad. The animals then described the drought on Earth.

"Rain is needed at once, Your Majesty," said the Toad, "or all living things on Earth will die!"

"I understand. Let there be rain on Earth this very moment!" ordered the King of Heaven.

Then, looking at the disorder of his court and his defeated subjects, the King shook his head and said to the Toad, "Uncle Toad, next time, when you need rain, you do not have to come all the way to these heavenly courts. Just croak, and I will know to send you rain."

The toad is a symbol of rain in Vietnam. When Uncle Toad croaks, rain will soon follow.